ID0605620

NO LONGER PROPERTY OF
SEATTLE PUBLIC LIBRARY

RECEIVED
NOV 02 2017
WALLINGFORD LIBRARY

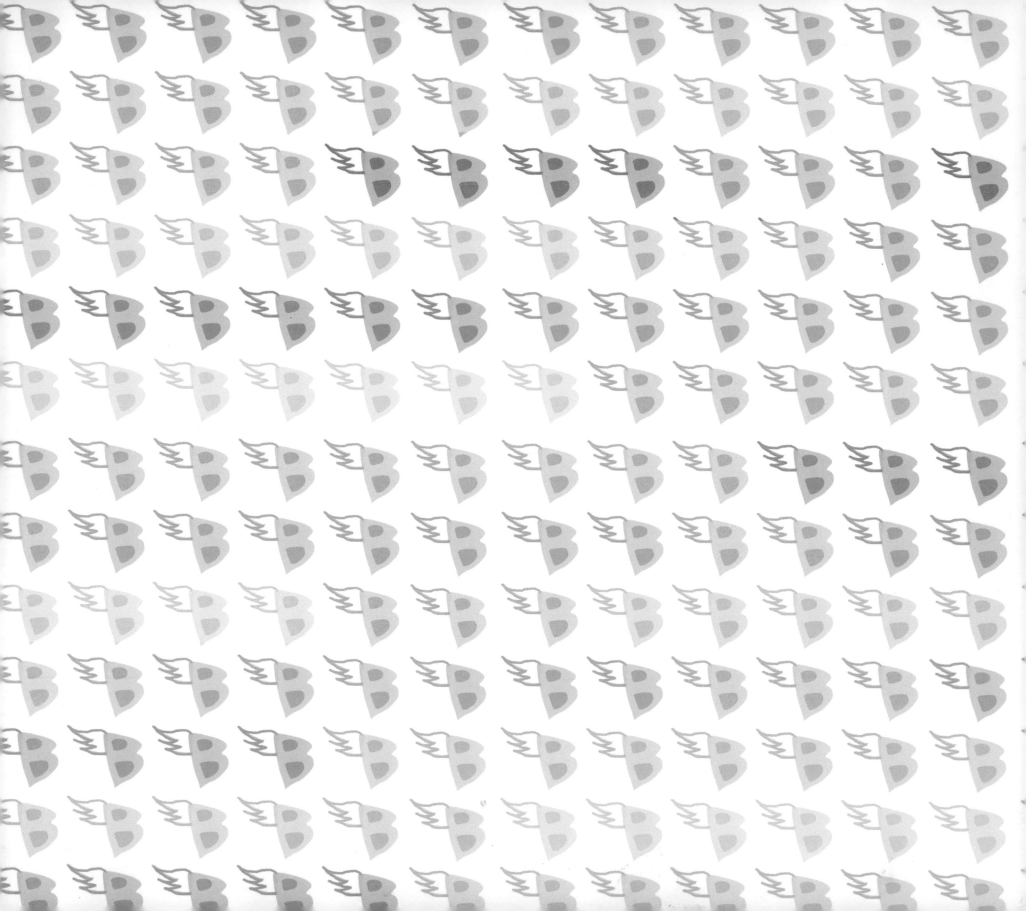

BRAVE

by Stacy McAnulty

illustrated by
Joanne Lew-Vriethoff

RP|KIDS
PHILADELPHIA

Text copyright © 2017 by Stacy McAnulty
Illustrations copyright © 2017 by Joanne Lew-Vriethoff

All rights reserved under the Pan-American and International Copyright Conventions

Printed in China

*This book may not be reproduced in whole or in part, in any form or by any means,
electronic or mechanical, including photocopying, recording, or by any information storage
and retrieval system now known or hereafter invented, without written permission from the publisher.*

Books published by Running Press are available at special discounts for bulk purchases
in the United States by corporations, institutions, and other organizations. For more information,
please contact the Special Markets Department at Perseus Books, 2300 Chestnut Street,
Suite 200, Philadelphia, PA 19103, or call (800) 810-4145, ext. 5000, or e-mail special.markets@perseusbooks.com.

ISBN 978-0-7624-5782-3
Library of Congress Control Number: 2016945288

9 8 7 6 5 4 3 2 1
Digit on the right indicates the number of this printing

Designed by T.L. Bonaddio
Edited by Lisa Cheng and Julie Matysik
Typography: Jolly Good Sans

Published by Running Press Kids,
An Imprint of Perseus Books, LLC,
A Subsidiary of Hachette Book Group, Inc.

Running Press Book Publishers
2300 Chestnut Street
Philadelphia, PA 19103–4371

Visit us on the web!
www.runningpress.com/rpkids

To Jen, Julie, Mabel & Penny—S. M.

Max & Mattiece, TYVM for your lovely art
To our next generation:
be Brave, be Fierce, be Bold, be True, be Kind,
be YOU . . . —J.L.V.

A brave kid ...

...seeks adventure.

A brave kid has super strength.

And a courageous heart.

A brave kid leads the team.

And never gives up.

A brave kid answers the call.

And fights the toughest battles.

A brave kid speaks for truth.

And stands for justice.

A brave kid gets back up.

And stays calm when others are afraid.

Brave kids can save the world.

Just by being . . .

... brave.

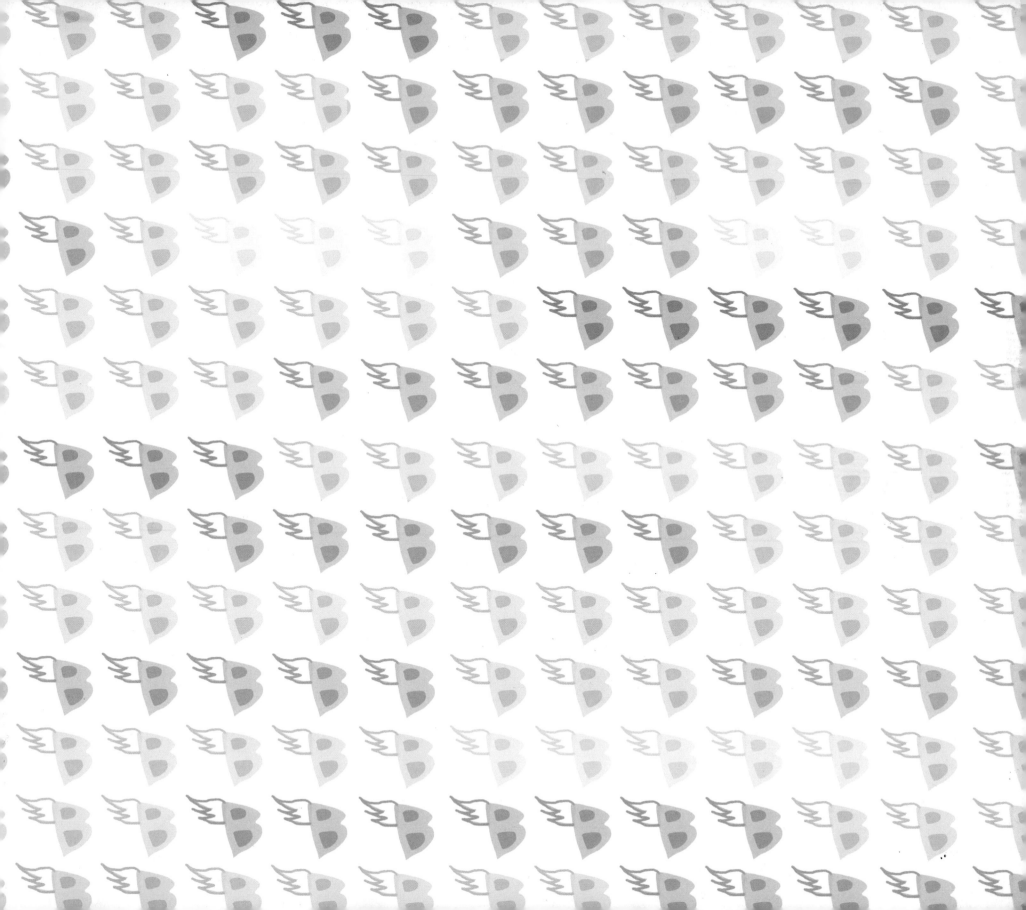